This Book Belongs To:

Charles R. Greene

The Muppet Babies live in a nursery
in a house on a street that is a lot like yours.
But they can travel anywhere anytime using a special power—
the power of the imagination.
Can you imagine what it would be like to go with them?
Join the Muppet Babies on this adventure and find out.

Weekly Reader Presents

Gonzo
Saves London Bridge

By Louise Gikow • Illustrated by Sue Venning

Muppet Press/Marvel • New York

"London Bridge is falling down, falling down, falling down. London Bridge is falling down, my fair lady!"

All the Muppet Babies fell down in a heap. All of them, that is, except Gonzo.

"Hey, Gonzo!" Kermit called. "Why don't you play, too?"

"Not me," said Gonzo, shaking his head. "I think it's a silly game. Everybody sings the same thing over and over again, and the bridge always falls down in the end."

"Gee," Kermit said, scratching his head. "I never thought of it that way. But it's still a lot of fun."

"If I had built London Bridge," Gonzo thought, "it wouldn't keep falling down. What's wrong with that bridge anyway?"

Gonzo looked down at his chicken, Camilla. "Do you want to go to London and find out?" he asked. Camilla looked as if she did. So Gonzo closed his eyes and imagined....

"Two tickets to London, please," Gonzo said.

"What names, sir?" asked the woman behind the ticket counter.

"Gonzo and Camilla."

"Aisle or window seat?"

"Window," Gonzo said. "Camilla has never flown before, and she'd like to see the view."

The first bridge Gonzo and Camilla saw in London was very old. But it was standing up. "That couldn't be it," Gonzo said.

"And that's not it, either." Gonzo shook his head as they walked past another bridge.

Gonzo and Camilla passed a lot of bridges, but none of them had fallen down. Then, in the distance, Gonzo saw something in the river. "That must be London Bridge!" he cried. "It's just like I imagined it would be!"

And there it was.

"It's a shame," sighed a London policeman. "The Royal Society of Bridge Builders can't figure out what to do to keep it standing up."

"Don't worry!" said Gonzo. "Camilla and I will fix it!"

Gonzo went over to the edge of the river where some small boats were docked.

"I've got a plan to keep London Bridge from falling down," he said to a boat captain. "Will you help?"

"Of course, mate!" said the captain. He and the other sailors listened to Gonzo's plan. Then they all got into their boats.

What do you imagine they did?

They used their boats to prop up London Bridge!

Unfortunately, there was a problem with Gonzo's plan. The boats kept floating down the river…and London Bridge went with them!

"Yipes!" said Gonzo. "Plan number two, coming up!"

Gonzo jumped into the river, where he found a whole family of whales. "Whales! Just what I need!" he thought happily.

"Hey, guys. Can you help me?" he asked them. The whales told him—in whale talk, of course—that they would be happy to oblige.

What do you imagine the whales did?

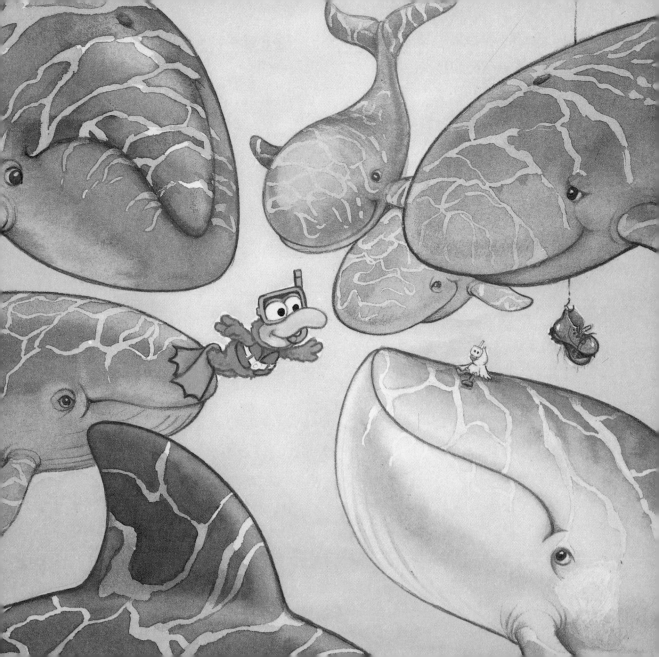

They spouted water from their spouts and held up
London Bridge!

But soon, the whales got tired, and before long,
London Bridge had fallen again.

Gonzo thought, and he thought. Then he had his
best idea yet.

He and Camilla called together all the children of
London and told them about the new plan. The children
thought it was a wonderful idea and agreed to help.

First, they went to a toy store. "We'd like five thousand
of these," Gonzo said to the storekeeper. "In all colors."

Then they stayed up all night long, working hard and
giggling the whole time. What do you imagine they did?

They tied thousands and thousands of balloons to
London Bridge.
    Gonzo's plan worked!

The citizens of London were very grateful to Gonzo. They gave him the key to the city. London Bridge would never fall down again!

"Gonzo! Gonzo!" a voice in the nursery called. "Wake up! We're going to draw some pictures now."

Gonzo looked up at Kermit and smiled. "That sounds great!" he said. "After all that excitement about London Bridge, Camilla needs something nice and quiet to do. Right, Camilla?"